Literary Laurels

Literary Laurels

A READER'S GUIDE TO AWARD-WINNING FICTION

Edited by

Laura Carlson
Sean Creighton
Sheila Cunningham

Hillyard
New York

Printed and bound in the United States of America.

10 9 8 7 6 5 4 3 2 1

ISBN 0-9647361-0-1

Introduction

Book lovers will love this book. *Literary Laurels* provides guidance in making reading choices by bringing together lists of the most distinguished fiction award winners of the last 90 years. Here's how it can help:

- You've had a bad day at the office and want to escape. Turn to the Edgar Allan Poe Award list for a compelling mystery.

- You're headed out West for vacation and want to get into the spirit of the place. Take along a selection from the Western Heritage Award list.

- Your reading tastes need a lift. Consult the Howells Medal and the Pulitzer Prize lists for what are deemed American "classics."

- You're completely stumped about what to read. Locate your favorite book or author on a list and read the rest.

Literary Laurels is a terrific present for Aunt Rita and will provide dozens of gift ideas for Uncle Hugo. Use it to expand your own reading horizons and to deepen your knowledge of literature. Or gather book information to dazzle your friends and excel on the trivia circuit.

Let this book be your handy check list or shopping list of more than 800 of the best fiction titles.

Contents

Contents

The ABBY Award

This award, whose name is an acronym for the American Booksellers Book of the Year, results from surveying thousands of booksellers for the book "they most love to recommend." Winners receive $5,000 plus a Tiffany crystal prism and a party when the award is presented at the American Booksellers Association annual convention each spring. The award was just launched in 1991, and the books often grace bestseller lists.

Adult Trade Category

1995   *Chicken Soup for the Soul,* Jack Canfield and Mark Victor Hansen*

1994   *Like Water for Chocolate,* Laura Esquivel

1993   *The Bridges of Madison County,* Robert James Waller

Children's Category

1995   *Rainbow Fish,* Marcus Pfister

1994   *Stellaluna,* Janell Cannon

1993   *Old Turtle,* Douglas Wood

1992   *Brother Eagle, Sister Sky: A Message from Chief Seattle,* Susan Jeffers

1991   *The Education of Little Tree,* Forrest Carter

*Nonfiction

The Agatha Award

This award is named in honor of the queen of mystery writing, Dame Agatha Christie, who wrote more than 70 thrilling novels. Agatha winners feature amateur sleuths and make for cozy reading. Its judges are the attendees at a mystery convention sponsored by Malice Domestic every spring. Winners receive a teapot.

1994   *She Walks These Hills*, Sharyn McCrumb

1993   *Dead Man's Island*, Carolyn Hart

1992   *Bootlegger's Daughter*, Margaret Maron

1991   *I.O.U.*, Nancy Pickard

1990   *Bum Steer*, Nancy Pickard

1989   *Naked Once More*, Elizabeth Peters

1988   *Something Wicked*, Carolyn Hart

The James Tait Black Memorial Prize

Started at the same time as America's Pulitzer Prize, this British equivalent honors the best book published in Great Britain each year. Or so says its lone judge, a Scottish university professor. Named for a partner in a venerable Edinburgh publishing firm, the award includes a prize of more than $2,000. This award, which has been overshadowed by the Booker Prize, is presented in April.

1994   *The Folding Star*, Alan Hollinghurst

1993   *Crossing the River*, Caryl Phillips

1992   *Sacred Country*, Rose Tremain

1991   *Downriver: or The Vessels of Wrath*, Ian Sinclair

1990   *Brazzaville Beach*, William Boyd

1989   *A Disaffection*, James Kelman

1988   *A Season in the West*, Piers Paul Read

1987   *The Golden Bird: Two Orkney Stories*, George Mackay Brown

1986   *Persephone*, Jenny Joseph

1985   *Winter Garden*, Robert Edric

1984   *Empire of the Sun*, J. G. Ballard

        Nights at the Circus, Angela Carter

1983   *Allegro Postillions*, Jonathan Keates

1982   *On the Black Hill*, Bruce Chatwin

1981   *Midnight's Children*, Salman Rushdie

        The Mosquito Coast, Paul Theroux

1980   *Waiting for the Barbarians*, J. M. Coetzee

1979   *Darkness Visible,* William Golding

1978   *Plumb,* Maurice Gee

1977   *The Honourable Schoolboy,* John Le Carré

1976   *Doctor Copernicus,* John Banville

1975   *The Great Victorian Collection,* Brian Moore

1974   *Monsieur, or The Prince of Darkness,* Lawrence Durrell

1973   *The Black Prince,* Iris Murdoch

1972   *G,* John Berger

1971   *A Guest of Honour,* Nadine Gordimer

1970   *The Bird of Paradise,* Lily Powell

1969   *Eva Trout,* Elizabeth Bowen

1968   *The Gasteropod,* Maggie Ross

1967   *Jerusalem the Golden,* Margaret Drabble

1966   *Such,* Christine Brooke-Rose

       Langrishe, Go Down, Aidan Higgins

1965   *The Mandelbaum Gate,* Muriel Spark

1964   *The Ice Saints,* Frank Tuohy

1963   *A Slanting Light,* Gerda Charles

1962   *Act of Destruction,* Ronald Hardy

1961   *The Ha-Ha,* Jennifer Dawson

1960   *Imperial Caesar,* Rex Warner

1959   *The Devil's Advocate,* Morris West

1958   *The Middle Age of Mrs. Eliot,* Angus Wilson

1957   *At Lady Molly's,* Anthony Powell

1956   *The Towers of Trebizond,* Rose Macauley

1955   *Mother and Son,* Ivy Compton-Burnett

1954   *The New Man* and *The Masters,* C. P. Snow

1953   *Troy Chimneys,* Margaret Kennedy

1952	*Men at Arms*, Evelyn Waugh
1951	*Father Goose*, W. C. Chapman-Mortimer
1950	*Along the Valley*, Robert Henriquez
1949	*The Far Cry*, Emma Smith
1948	*The Heart of the Matter*, Graham Greene
1947	*Eustace and Hilda*, L. P. Hartley
1946	*Poor Man's Tapestry*, G. Oliver Onions
1945	*Travellers*, L. A. G. Strong
1944	*Young Tom*, Forrest Reid
1943	*Tales from Bectine Bridge*, Mary Lavin
1942	*Monkey* (by Wu Ch'eng-en), Arthur Whaley
1941	*A House of Children*, Joyce Cary
1940	*The Voyage*, Charles Morgan
1939	*After Many a Summer Dies the Swan*, Aldous Huxley
1938	*A Ship of the Line* and *Flying Colours*, C. S. Forester
1937	*Highland River*, Neil M. Gunn
1936	*South Riding*, Winifred Holtby
1935	*The Root and the Flower*, L. H. Myers
1934	*I, Claudius* and *Claudius the God*, Robert Graves
1933	*England, Their England*, A. G. Macdonell
1932	*Boomerang*, Helen Simpson
1931	*Without My Cloak*, Kate O'Brien
1930	*Miss Mole*, E. H. Young
1929	*The Good Companions*, J. B. Priestley
1928	*Memoirs of a Fox-Hunting Man*, Siegfried Sassoon
1927	*Portrait of Clare*, Francis Brett Young
1926	*Adam's Breed*, Radclyffe Hall
1925	*The Informer*, Liam O'Flaherty

1924   *A Passage to India,* E. M. Forster

1923   *Riceyman Steps,* Arnold Bennett

1922   *Lady into Fox,* David Garnett

1921   *Memoirs of a Midget,* Walter de la Mare

1920   *The Lost Girl,* D. H. Lawrence

1919   *The Secret City,* Hugh Walpole

The Booker Prize

This well-heralded British award has attracted controversy in recent years for its tendency to applaud contemporary obsessions and often impenetrable writing. It considers any fiction written in the Commonwealth, Republic of Ireland, or South Africa. Sponsored by the British food conglomerate of the same name, the award now bestows the equivalent of $30,000 and is granted by a committee of authors. Established in 1969, the award has been credited with prompting a fivefold increase in book sales.

1994   *How Late It Was, How Late*, James Kelman

1993   *Paddy Clarke Ha Ha Ha*, Roddy Doyle

1992   *The English Patient*, Michael Ondaatje

        Sacred Hunger, Barry Unsworth

1991   *The Famished Road*, Ben Okri

1990   *Possession*, A. S. Byatt

1989   *The Remains of the Day*, Kazuo Ishiguro

1988   *Oscar and Lucinda*, Peter Carey

1987   *Moon Tiger*, Penelope Lively

1986   *The Old Devils*, Kingsley Amis

1985   *The Bone People*, Keri Hulme

1984   *Hotel du Lac*, Anita Brookner

1983   *Life & Times of Michael K*, J. M. Coetzee

1982   *Schindler's Ark*, Thomas Keneally (published in the U.S. as *Schindler's List*)

1981   *Midnight's Children*, Salman Rushdie

1980   *Rites of Passage*, William Golding

1979   *Offshore*, Penelope Fitzgerald

1978 *The Sea, The Sea,* Iris Murdoch

1977 *Staying On,* Paul Scott

1976 *Saville,* David Storey

1975 *Heat and Dust,* Ruth Prawer Jhabvala

1974 *The Conservationist,* Nadine Gordimer
      Holiday, Stanley Middleton

1973 *The Siege of Krishnapur,* J. G. Farrell

1972 *G,* John Berger

1971 *In a Free State,* V. S. Naipaul

1970 *The Elected Member,* Bernice Rubens

1969 *Something to Answer For,* P. H. Newby

The Booker Prize Shortlist

Runners-up for the Booker Prize reap handsome gains from their close finish through higher book sales. Readers of these finalists will find comparable quality to the Booker Prize list. Due to the large numbers of runners-up, titles from only the last ten years are included here.

1994   *Beside the Ocean of Time*, George Mackay Brown
       The Folding Star, Alan Hollinghurst
       Reef, Romesh Gunesekera
       Paradise, Abdulrazak Gurnah
       Knowledge of Angels, Jill Paton Walsh
1993   *Under the Frog*, Tibor Fischer
       Scar Tissue, Michael Ignatieff
       Remembering Babylon, David Malouf
       Crossing the River, Caryl Phillips
       The Stone Diaries, Carol Shields
1992   *Serenity House*, Christopher Hope
       The Butcher Boy, Patrick McCabe
       Black Dogs, Ian McEwan
       Daughters of the House, Michèle Roberts
1991   *Time's Arrow*, Martin Amis
       The Van, Roddy Doyle
       Such a Long Journey, Rohinton Mistry
       The Redundancy of Courage, Timothy Mo
       Two Lives, William Trevor

1990   *An Awfully Big Adventure,* Beryl Bainbridge
           The Gate of Angels, Penelope Fitzgerald
           Amongst Women, John McGahern
           Lies of Silence, Brian Moore
           Solomon Gursky Was Here, Mordecai Richler

1989   *Cat's Eye,* Margaret Atwood
           The Book of Evidence, John Banville
           Jigsaw, Sybille Bedford
           A Disaffection, James Kelman
           Restoration, Rose Tremain

1988   *Utz,* Bruce Chatwin
           The Beginning of Spring, Penelope Fitzgerald
           Nice Work, David Lodge
           The Satanic Verses, Salman Rushdie
           The Lost Father, Marina Warner

1987   *Anthills of the Savannah,* Chinua Achebe
           Chatterton, Peter Ackroyd
           Circles of Deceit, Nina Bawden
           The Colour of Blood, Brian Moore
           The Book and the Brotherhood, Iris Murdoch

1986   *The Handmaid's Tale,* Margaret Atwood
           Gabriel's Lament, Paul Bailey
           What's Bred in the Bone, Robertson Davies
           An Artist of the Floating World, Kazuo Ishiguro
           An Insular Possession, Timothy Mo

1985   *Illywhacker,* Peter Carey
           The Battle of Pollocks Crossing, J. L. Carr
           The Good Terrorist, Doris Lessing

Last Letters from Hav, Jan Morris

The Good Apprentice, Iris Murdoch

1984 *Empire of the Sun,* J. G. Ballard

Flaubert's Parrot, Julian Barnes

In Custody, Anita Desai

According to Mark, Penelope Lively

Small World, David Lodge

The Caldecott Medal

Children's picture books are celebrated by this award, which is administered by the American Library Association. It is named for the English illustrator Randolph Caldecott, who authored and illustrated *The House That Jack Built* among other well-loved works. Announced in February, the award is given for the most distinguished American picture book and is considered one of the highest achievements in children's literature.

1994   *Smoky Night*, Eve Bunting, illus. by David Diaz

1993   *Mirette on the High Wire*, Emily Arnold McCully

1992   *Tuesday*, David Wiesner

1991   *Black and White*, David Macaulay

1990   *Lon Po Po: A Red-Riding Hood Story from China*, trans. and illus. by Ed Young

1989   *Song and Dance Man*, Karen Ackerman, illus. by Stephen Gammell

1988   *Owl Moon*, Jane Yolen, illus. by John Schoenherr

1987   *Hey, Al*, Arthur Yorinks, illus. by Richard Egielski

1986   *The Polar Express*, Chris Van Allsburg

1985   *Saint George and the Dragon*, retold by Margaret Hodges, illus. by Trina Schart Hyman

1984   *The Glorious Flight: Across the Channel with Louis Bleriot*, Alice Provensen and Martin Provensen

1983   *Shadow*, Blaise Cendrars, trans. and illus. by Marcia Brown

1982   *Jumanji*, Chris Van Allsburg

1981   *Fables*, Arnold Lobel

1980   *Ox-Cart Man*, Donald Hall, pictures by Barbara Cooney

1979   *The Girl Who Loved Wild Horses,* Paul Goble

1978   *Noah's Ark,* Peter Spier

1977   *Ashanti to Zulu,* Margaret Musgrove, pictures by Leo
       Dillon and Diane Dillon

1976   *Why Mosquitoes Buzz in People's Ears,* retold by Verna
       Aardema, pictures by Leo Dillon and Diane Dillon

1975   *Arrow to the Sun,* Gerald McDermott

1974   *Duffy and the Devil,* retold by Harve Zemach, pictures by
       Margot Zemach

1973   *The Funny Little Woman,* retold by Arlene Mosel, illus. by
       Blair Lent

1972   *One Fine Day,* Nonny Hogrogian

1971   *A Story A Story,* Gail E. Haley

1970   *Sylvester and the Magic Pebble,* William Steig

1969   *The Fool of the World and the Flying Ship,* retold by Arthur
       Ransome, illus. by Uri Shulevitz

1968   *Drummer Hoff,* adapted by Barbara Emberley, illus. by Ed
       Emberley

1967   *Sam, Bangs & Moonshine,* Evaline Ness

1966   *Always Room for One More,* Sorche Nic Leodhas, illus. by
       Nonny Hogrogian

1965   *May I Bring a Friend,* Beatrice Schenk de Regniers, illus.
       by Beni Montresor

1964   *Where the Wild Things Are,* Maurice Sendak

1963   *The Snowy Day,* Ezra Jack Keats

1962   *Once a Mouse,* Marcia Brown

1961   *Baboushka and the Three Kings,* Ruth Robbins, illus. by
       Nicolas Sidjakov

1960   *Nine Days to Christmas,* Marie Hall Ets and Aurora
       Labastida

1959   *Chanticleer and the Fox,* Barbara Cooney

The Edgar Allan Poe Award

Known as the "Edgar," this award lauds great suspense, detective, and spy works. Named for the writer of such chilling stories and poetry as the "The Tell-Tale Heart" and "The Raven," the award was first granted in 1954. Its judges are the members of the Mystery Writers of America. The winner is presented with a ceramic bust of Poe at the Mystery Writers' spring convention.

1995   *The Red Scream,* Mary Willis Walker

1994   *The Sculptress,* Minette Walters

1993   *Bootlegger's Daughter,* Margaret Maron

1992   *A Dance at the Slaughterhouse,* Lawrence Block

1991   *New Orleans Mourning,* Julie Smith

1990   *Black Cherry Blues,* James Lee Burke

1989   *A Cold Red Sunrise,* Stuart M. Kaminsky

1988   *Old Bones,* Aaron Elkins

1987   *A Dark-Adapted Eye,* Barbara Vine

1986   *The Suspect,* L. R. Wright

1985   *Briarpatch,* Ross Thomas

1984   *La Brava,* Elmore Leonard

1983   *Billingsgate Shoal,* Rick Boyer

1982   *Peregrine,* William Bayer

1981   *Whip Hand,* Dick Francis

1980   *The Rheingold Route,* Arthur Maling

1979   *The Eye of the Needle,* Ken Follett

1978   *Catch Me: Kill Me,* William Hallahan

1977   *Promised Land,* Robert Parker

1976	*Hopscotch,* Brian Garfield
1975	*Peter's Pence,* Jon Cleary
1974	*Dance Hall of the Dead,* Tony Hillerman
1973	*The Lingala Code,* Warren Kiefer
1972	*The Day of the Jackal,* Frederick Forsyth
1971	*The Laughing Policeman,* Maj. Sjowall and Per Wahloo
1970	*Forfeit,* Dick Francis
1969	*A Case of Need,* Jeffery Hudson
1968	*God Save the Mark,* Donald E. Westlake
1967	*King of the Rainy Country,* Nicolas Freeling
1966	*The Quiller Memorandum,* Adam Hall
1965	*The Spy Who Came in from the Cold,* John Le Carré
1964	*The Light of Day,* Eric Ambler
1963	*Death of the Joyful Woman,* Ellis Peters
1962	*Gideon's Fire,* J. J. Marric
1961	*Progress of a Crime,* Julian Symons
1960	*The Hours Before Dawn,* Celia Fremlin
1959	*The Eighth Circle,* Stanley Ellin
1958	*Room to Swing,* Ed Lacy
1957	*A Dram of Poison,* Charlotte Armstrong
1956	*Beast in View,* Margaret Millar
1955	*The Long Goodbye,* Raymond Chandler
1954	*Beat Not the Bones,* Charlotte Jay

The PEN/Faulkner Award

This award, administered by PEN (Poets, Playwrights, Editors, Essayists, and Novelists), gives writers the chance to honor their peers by serving as judges. This is a 1980 revival of an award started by Southern writer William Faulkner with his 1949 Nobel Prize money. Candidates are judged by three American writers of fiction. Before selecting the winner, the judges read more than 250 works. The winning author receives $15,000 in May.

1995   *Snow Falling on Cedars*, David Guterson

1994   *Operation Shylock*, Philip Roth

1993   *Postcards*, E. Annie Proulx

1992   *Mao II*, Don DeLillo

1991   *Philadelphia Fire*, John Edgar Wideman

1990   *Billy Bathgate*, E. L. Doctorow

1989   *Dusk*, James Salter

1988   *World's End*, T. Coraghessan Boyle

1987   *Soldiers in Hiding*, Richard Wiley

1986   *The Old Forest...*, Peter Taylor

1985   *The Barracks Thief*, Tobias Wolff

1984   *Sent for You Yesterday*, John Edgar Wideman

1983   *Seaview*, Toby Olson

1982   *The Chaneysville Incident*, David Bradley

1981   *How German Is It?*, Walter Abish

The Ernest Hemingway
Foundation Award

This award honors a first-published work by an American writer. It is named for Ernest Hemingway, a highly original and much-imitated American writer who won both the Pulitzer and Nobel prizes in the mid-fifties. Judges are writers recommended by PEN (Poets, Playwrights, Editors, Essayists, and Novelists), and appear to favor distinctive writing styles. The winner receives a cash prize of $7,500 in the spring.

1995   *The Grass Dancer,* Susan Power

1994   *The Magic of Blood,* Dagoberto Gilb

1993   *Lost in the City,* Edward P. Jones

1992   *Wartime Lies,* Louis Begley

1991   *Maps to Anywhere,* Bernard Cooper

1990   *The Ice at the Bottom of the World,* Mark Richard

1989   *The Book of Ruth,* Jane Hamilton

1988   *Imagining Argentina,* Lawrence Thornton

1987   *Tongues of Flame,* Mary Ward Brown

1986   *Lady's Time,* Alan V. Hewat

1985   *Dreams of Sleep,* Josephine Humphreys

1984   *During the Reign of the Queen of Persia,* Joan Chase

1983   *Shiloh and Other Stories,* Bobbie Ann Mason

1982   *Housekeeping,* Marilynne Robinson

1981   *Household Words,* Joan Silber

1980   *Mom Kills Kids and Self,* Alan Saperstein

1979   *Hasen,* Reuben Bercovitch

1978   *A Way of Life, Like Any Other,* Darcy O'Brien

1977   *Speedboat,* Renata Adler

1976   *Parthian Shot,* Loyd Little

The Howells Medal

A winner is selected every five years by a committee drawn from the elite membership of the American Academy of Arts and Letters. The medal is named in honor of William Dean Howells, who was one of the founding members of the Academy along with Mark Twain. Howells was revered for his realistic portrayals of post–Civil War life in New England. First presented in 1925, the medal commends either one book or the entire work of some of America's most distinguished writers. It is bestowed in late spring.

1990	*Billy Bathgate,* E. L. Doctorow
1985	No award
1980	*So Long, See You Tomorrow,* William Maxwell
1975	*Gravity's Rainbow,* Thomas Pynchon
1970	*The Confessions of Nat Turner,* William Styron
1965	*The Wapshot Scandal,* John Cheever
1960	*By Love Possessed,* James Gould Cozzens
1955	*The Ponder Heart,* Eudora Welty
1950	William Faulkner
1945	Booth Tarkington
1940	Ellen Glasgow
1935	*The Good Earth,* Pearl S. Buck
1930	*Death Comes for the Archbishop,* Willa Cather
1925	Mary E. Wilkins Freeman

The Hugo Award

The oldest science fiction award, the Hugo promotes tales of futuristic lands where life is driven by science and technology. Named after Hugo Gernsback, a major writer and spokesman for this genre, the award is granted by popular vote of the 10,000-member World Science Fiction Society. A trophy is presented in late summer at the society's annual convention.

1994   *Green Mars*, Kim Stanley Robinson

1993   *A Fire Upon the Deep*, Vernor Vinge

        Doomsday Book, Connie Willis

1992   *Barrayar*, Lois McMaster Bujold

1991   *The Vor Game*, Lois McMaster Bujold

1990   *Hyperion*, Dan Simmons

1989   *Cyteen*, C. J. Cherryh

1988   *The Uplift War*, David Brin

1987   *Speaker for the Dead*, Orson Scott Card

1986   *Ender's Game*, Orson Scott Card

1985   *Neuromancer*, William Gibson

1984   *Startide Rising*, David Brin

1983   *Foundation's Edge*, Isaac Asimov

1982   *Downbelow Station*, C. J. Cherryh

1981   *The Snow Queen*, Joan D. Vinge

1980   *The Fountains of Paradise*, Arthur C. Clarke

1979   *Dreamsnake*, Vonda McIntyre

1978   *Gateway*, Frederik Pohl

1977   *Where Late the Sweet Birds Sang*, Kate Wilhelm

1976   *The Forever War,* Joe Haldeman

1975   *The Dispossessed,* Ursula K. Le Guin

1974   *Rendezvous with Rama,* Arthur C. Clarke

1973   *The Gods Themselves,* Isaac Asimov

1972   *To Your Scattered Bodies Go,* Philip Jose Farmer

1971   *Ringworld,* Larry Niven

1970   *The Left Hand of Darkness,* Ursula K. Le Guin

1969   *Stand on Zanzibar,* John Brunner

1968   *Lord of Light,* Roger Zelazny

1967   *The Moon Is a Harsh Mistress,* Robert A. Heinlein

1966   *...And Call Me Conrad* (also titled *This Immortal*), Roger Zelazny

       Dune, Frank Herbert

1965   *The Wanderer,* Fritz Leiber

1964   *Here Gather the Stars* (also titled *Way Station*), Clifford D. Simak

1963   *The Man in the High Castle,* Philip K. Dick

1962   *Stranger in a Strange Land,* Robert A. Heinlein

1961   *A Canticle for Leibowitz,* Walter M. Miller, Jr.

1960   *Starship Troopers,* Robert A. Heinlein

1959   *A Case of Conscience,* James Blish

1958   *The Big Time,* Fritz Leiber

1957   No award

1956   *Double Star,* Robert A. Heinlein

1955   *They'd Rather Be Right,* Mark Clifton and Frank Riley

1954   No award

1953   *The Demolished Man,* Alfred Bester

The Sue Kaufman Prize for First Fiction

This award was established by the American Academy of Arts and Letters in memory of the novelist and short story writer Sue Kaufman. She is best known for *The Diary of a Mad Housewife*, a comic portrayal of contemporary neuroses. Given annually, the award honors the best first novel. Academy judges appear to favor offbeat plots and characters when choosing a winner. A cash prize of $2,500 is presented in May.

1994   *In the Sparrow Hills*, Emile Capouya

1993   *The Long Night of White Chickens*, Francisco Goldman

1992   *Afghanistan*, Alex Ullmann

1991   *The Quincunx*, Charles Palliser

1990   *Oldest Living Confederate Widow Tells All*, Allan Gurganus

1989   *The Garden State*, Gary Krist

1988   *Ellen Foster*, Kaye Gibbons

1987   *The All of It*, Jeannette Haien

1986   *Face*, Cecile Pineda

1985   *Love Medicine*, Louise Erdrich

1984   *Angels*, Denis Johnson

1983   *My Old Sweetheart*, Susanna Moore

1982   *Easy Travel to Other Planets*, Ted Mooney

1981   *Guys Like Us*, Tom Lorenz

1980   *Black Tickets*, Jayne Anne Phillips

The *Los Angeles Times* Book Prize

Eligibility for this award is worldwide as long as the book is published in English. Three judges appointed by the *Los Angeles Times* appear to favor stories about people trying to liberate themselves from political or psychological oppression. Established in 1980, the award is a $1,000 cash prize given in November.

1994   *Remembering Babylon,* David Malouf

1993   *Pigs in Heaven,* Barbara Kingsolver

1992   *Maus II, A Survivor's Tale: And Here My Troubles Began,* Art Spiegelman

1991   *White People,* Allan Gurganus

1990   *Lantern Slides,* Edna O'Brien

1989   *The Heart of the Country,* Fay Weldon

1988   *Love in the Time of Cholera,* Gabriel Garcia Marquez

1987   *Fools Crow,* James Welch

1986   *The Handmaid's Tale,* Margaret Atwood

1985   *Love Medicine,* Louise Erdrich

1984   *The Unbearable Lightness of Being,* Milan Kundera

1983   *Schindler's List,* Thomas Keneally

1982   *A Flag for Sunrise,* Robert Stone

1981   *The White Hotel,* D. M. Thomas

1980   *The Second Coming,* Walker Percy

The National Book Award

This award is the central feature of the National Book Foundation's efforts to promote reading in America through author events and fund-raising for literacy programs. Winning novels often become American classics. The books capture contemporary life, interests, and problems across the nation. Presented in November, winners receive $10,000.

1994   *A Frolic of His Own*, William Gaddis

1993   *The Shipping News*, E. Annie Proulx

1992   *All the Pretty Horses*, Cormac McCarthy

1991   *Mating*, Norman Rush

1990   *Middle Passage*, Charles Johnson

1989   *Spartina*, John Casey

1988   *Paris Trout*, Pete Dexter

1987   *Paco's Story*, Larry Heinemann

1986   *World's Fair*, E. L. Doctorow

1985   *White Noise*, Don DeLillo

1984   *Victory Over Japan: A Book of Stories*, Ellen Gilchrist

1983   *The Color Purple*, Alice Walker

1982   *Rabbit Is Rich*, John Updike

1981   *Plains Song*, Wright Morris

1980   *Sophie's Choice*, William Styron

1979   *Going After Cacciato*, Tim O'Brien

1978   *Blood Ties*, Mary Lee Settle

1977   *The Spectator Bird*, Wallace Stegner

1976   *J R*, William Gaddis

1975   *Dog Soldiers,* Robert Stone

      The Hair of Harold Roux, Thomas Williams

1974   *Gravity's Rainbow,* Thomas Pynchon

      A Crown of Feathers and Other Stories, Isaac Bashevis Singer

1973   *Chimera,* John Barth

      Augustus, John Williams

1972   *The Complete Stories of Flannery O'Connor,* Flannery O'Connor

1971   *Mr. Sammler's Planet,* Saul Bellow

1970   *Them,* Joyce Carol Oates

1969   *Steps,* Jerzy Kosinski

1968   *The Eighth Day,* Thornton Wilder

1967   *The Fixer,* Bernard Malamud

1966   *The Collected Stories of Katherine Anne Porter,* Katherine Ann Porter

1965   *Herzog,* Saul Bellow

1964   *The Centaur,* John Updike

1963   *Morte D'Urban,* J. F. Powers

1962   *The Moviegoer,* Walker Percy

1961   *The Waters of Kronos,* Conrad Richter

1960   *Goodbye, Columbus,* Philip Roth

1959   *The Magic Barrel,* Bernard Malamud

1958   *The Wapshot Chronicle,* John Cheever

1957   *The Field of Vision,* Wright Morris

1956   *Ten North Frederick,* John O'Hara

1955   *A Fable,* William Faulkner

1954   *The Adventures of Augie March,* Saul Bellow

1953   *Invisible Man,* Ralph Ellison

The National Book Award Finalists

Finalists for the National Book Award receive a cash prize of $1,000. Due to the large number of runners-up, finalists for only ten years are included here.

1994   *Moses Supposes,* Ellen Currie
       White Man's Grave, Richard Dooling
       The Bird Artist, Howard Norman
       The Collected Stories, Grace Paley
1993   *Come to Me,* Amy Bloom
       The Pugilist at Rest, Thom Jones
       Operation Wandering Soul, Richard Powers
       Swimming in the Volcano, Bob Schacochis
1992   *Bastard out of Carolina,* Dorothy Allison
       Dreaming in Cuban, Cristina Garcia
       Lost in the City, Edward P. Jones
       Outerbridge Reach, Robert Stone
1991   *Wartime Lies,* Louis Begley
       Frog, Stephen Dixon
       The Macguffin, Stanley Elkin
       Beyond Deserving, Sandra Scofield
1990   *Chromos,* Felipe Alfau
       Paradise, Elena Castedo
       Dogeaters, Jessica Hagedorn
       Because It Is Bitter, and Because It Is My Heart, Joyce Carol Oates

1989   *Billy Bathgate*, E. L. Doctorow
        Geek Love, Katherine Dunn
        The Mambo Kings Play Songs of Love, Oscar Hijuelos
        The Joy Luck Club, Amy Tan
1988   *Libra*, Don DeLillo
        Vanished, Mary McGarry Morris
        Wheat That Springeth Green, James F. Powers
        Breathing Lessons, Anne Tyler
1987   *That Night*, Alice McDermott
        Beloved, Toni Morrison
        The Northern Lights, Howard Norman
        The Counterlife, Philip Roth
1986   *Whites*, Norman Rush
        A Summons to Memphis, Peter Taylor
1985   *Always Coming Home*, Ursula K. Le Guin
        The Tree of Life, Hugh Nissenson
1984   *Foreign Affairs*, Alison Lurie
        The Anatomy Lesson, Philip Roth

The National Book Critics Circle Award

This is the critics' choice among book-length fiction. The Critics Circle comprises 580 professional book critics and book review editors. Works recognized by these book reviewers are often written by established authors with a following. Since 1975, a scroll and citation have been awarded to winners in March.

1994   *The Stone Diaries,* Carol Shields

1993   *A Lesson Before Dying,* Ernest J. Gaines

1992   *All the Pretty Horses,* Cormac McCarthy

1991   *A Thousand Acres,* Jane Smiley

1990   *Rabbit at Rest,* John Updike

1989   *Billy Bathgate,* E. L Doctorow

1988   *The Middleman and Other Stories,* Bharati Mukherjee

1987   *The Counterlife,* Philip Roth

1986   *Kate Vaiden,* Reynolds Price

1985   *The Accidental Tourist,* Anne Tyler

1984   *Love Medicine,* Louise Erdrich

1983   *Ironweed,* William Kennedy

1982   *George Mills,* Stanley Elkin

1981   *Rabbit Is Rich,* John Updike

1980   *The Transit of Venus,* Shirley Hazzard

1979   *The Year of the French,* Thomas Flanagan

1978   *The Stories of John Cheever,* John Cheever

1977   *Song of Solomon,* Toni Morrison

1976   *October Light,* John Gardner

1975   *Ragtime,* E. L. Doctorow

The National Jewish Book Award

How does being Jewish affect a person's life? The National Jewish Book Award is given to the book or collection of stories that best addresses that theme, according to the Jewish Book Council. Established in 1948, an award of $750 is given each November for the outstanding book written by a citizen of the United States, Canada, or Israel.

1994   *The Prince of West End Avenue*, Alan Isler

1993   *Mr. Mani*, A. B. Yehoshua

1992   *The Rosendorf Quartet*, Nathan Shaham

1991   *The Gift of Asher Lev*, Chaim Potok

1990   *Five Seasons*, A. B. Yehoshua

1989   *The Immortal Bartfuss*, Aharon Appelfeld

1988   *The Counterlife*, Philip Roth

1987   No award

1986   *The Unloved: From the Diary of Perla S.*, Arnost Lustig

1985   *Invisible Mending*, Frederick Busch

1984   *An Admirable Woman*, Arthur A. Cohen

1983   *Temple*, Robert Greenfield

1982   No award

1981   *Ellis Island and Other Stories*, Mark Helprin

        O, My America!, Johanna Kaplan

1980   *Apathetic Bookie Joint*, Daniel Fuchs

1979   *Leah's Journey*, Gloria Goldreich

1978   *The Yeshiva, Vol. I and II*, Chaim Grade

1977   *Bloodshed and Three Novellas*, Cynthia Ozick

1976   *Other People's Lives*, Johanna Kaplan

1975   *White Eagle, Dark Skies*, Jean Karsavina

1974   *Judah the Pious*, Francine Prose

1973   *Somewhere Else*, Robert Kotlowitz

1972   *The Pagan Rabbi and Other Stories*, Cynthia Ozick

1971   No award

1970   *Waiting for the News*, Leo Litwak

1969   *Memory of Autumn*, Charles Angoff

1968   No award

1967   *The Well*, Chaim Grade

1966   *The Stronghold*, Meyer Levin

1965   *The Town Beyond the Well*, Elie Wiesel

1964   *The King's Persons*, Joanne Greenberg

1963   *The Slave*, Isaac Bashevis Singer

1962   *Wedding Band*, Samuel Yellen

1961   *The Human Season*, Edward L. Wallant

1960   *Goodbye, Columbus*, Philip Roth

1959   *Exodus*, Leon Uris

1958   *The Assistant*, Bernard Malamud

1957   *Raquel: The Jewess of Toledo*, Leon Feuchtwanger

1956   No award

1955   *Blessed Is the Land*, Louis Zara

1954   *In the Morning Light*, Charles Angoff

1953   *The Juggler*, Michael Blankfort

1952   *Quiet Street*, Zelda Popkin

1951   *The Testament of the Lost Son*, Soma Morgenstern

1950   *The Wall*, John Hersey

1949   *My Glorious Brothers*, Howard Fast

The Nebula Award

The Science-fiction and Fantasy Writers of America, a group of more than 1,800 published authors, established this award in 1965. Each year members pool their personal favorites and together select the best book to be honored in the spring. There are significant overlaps with the Hugo Award.

1994   *Red Mars*, Kim Stanley Robinson

1993   *Doomsday Book*, Connie Willis

1992   *Stations of the Tide*, Michael Swanwick

1991   *Tehanu: The Last Book of Earthsea*, Ursula K. Le Guin

1990   *The Healer's War*, Elizabeth Ann Scarborough

1989   *Falling Free*, Lois McMaster Bujold

1988   *The Falling Woman*, Pat Murphy

1987   *Speaker for the Dead*, Orson Scott Card

1986   *Ender's Game*, Orson Scott Card

1985   *Neuromancer*, William Gibson

1984   *Startide Rising*, David Brin

1983   *No Enemy But Time*, Michael Bishop

1982   *The Claw of the Conciliator*, Gene Wolfe

1981   *Timescape*, Gregory Benford

1980   *The Fountains of Paradise*, Arthur C. Clarke

1979   *Dreamsnake*, Vonda N. McIntyre

1978   *Gateway*, Frederik Pohl

1977   *Man Plus*, Frederik Pohl

1976   *The Forever War*, Joe W. Haldeman

1975	*The Dispossessed,* Ursula K. Le Guin
1974	*Rendezvous with Rama,* Arthur C. Clarke
1973	*The Gods Themselves,* Isaac Asimov
1972	*A Time of Changes,* Robert Silvberg
1971	*Ringworld,* Larry Niven
1970	*The Left Hand of Darkness,* Ursula K. Le Guin
1969	*Rite of Passage,* Alexei Pansin
1968	*The Einstein Intersection,* Samuel R. Delany
1967	*Babel-17,* Samuel R. Delany
	Flowers for Algernon, Daniel Keyes
1966	*Dune,* Frank Herbert

The Newbery Medal

Like the Caldecott Medal, this children's book award is administered by the American Library Association. It is named for the Englishman, John Newbery, who was the first publisher and seller of children's books. Starting in 1922, a medal has been awarded to the best American writer in this category each February.

1995   *Walk Two Moons,* Sharon Creech

1994   *The Giver,* Lois Lowry

1993   *Missing May,* Cynthia Rylant

1992   *Shiloh,* Phyllis Reynolds Naylor

1991   *Maniac Magee,* Jerry Spinelli

1990   *Number the Stars,* Lois Lowry

1989   *Joyful Noise: Poems for Two Voices,* Paul Fleischman

1988   *Lincoln: A Photobiography,* Russell Freedman

1987   *The Whipping Boy,* Sid Fleischman

1986   *Sarah, Plain and Tall,* Patricia MacLachlan

1985   *The Hero and the Crown,* Robin McKinley

1984   *Dear Mr. Henshaw,* Beverly Cleary

1983   *Dicey's Song,* Cynthia Voigt

1982   *A Visit to William Blake's Inn: Poems for Innocent and Experienced Travelers,* Nancy Willard

1981   *Jacob Have I Loved,* Katherine Paterson

1980   *A Gathering of Days,* Joan Blos

1979   *The Westing Game,* Ellen Raskin

1978   *Bridge to Terabithia,* Katherine Paterson

1977   *Roll of Thunder, Hear My Cry,* Mildred D. Taylor

1976   *Grey King,* Susan Cooper

1975   *M. C. Higgins the Great*, Virginia Hamilton

1974   *The Slave Dancer*, Paula Fox

1973   *Julie of the Wolves*, Jean Craighead George

1972   *Mrs. Frisby and the Rats of NIMH*, Robert C. O'Brien

1971   *The Summer of the Swans*, Betsy Byars

1970   *Sounder*, William H. Armstrong

1969   *The High King*, Lloyd Alexander

1968   *From the Mixed-Up Files of Mrs. Basil E. Frankweiler*, E.L. Konigsburg

1967   *Up a Road Slowly*, Irene Hunt

1966   *I, Juan de Pareja*, Elizabeth Borton de Trevino

1965   *Shadow of a Bull*, Maja Wojciechowska

1964   *It's Like This, Cat*, Emily Cheney Neville

1963   *A Wrinkle in Time*, Madeleine L'Engle

1962   *The Bronze Bow*, Elizabeth George Speare

1961   *Island of the Blue Dolphins*, Scott O'Dell

1960   *Onion John*, Joseph Krumgold

1959   *The Witch of Blackbird Pond*, Elizabeth George Speare

1958   *Rifles for Watie*, Harold Keith

1957   *Miracles on Maple Hill*, Virginia Sorensen

1956   *Carry On, Mr. Bowditch*, Jean Lee Latham

1955   *The Wheel on the School*, Meindert DeJong

1954   *...And Now Miguel*, Joseph Krumgold

1953   *Secret of the Andes*, Ann Nolan Clark

1952   *Ginger Pye*, Eleanor Estes

1951   *Amos Fortune, Free Man*, Elizabeth Yates

1950   *The Door in the Wall*, Marguerite de Angeli

1949   *King of the Wind*, Marguerite Henry

The Newbery Medal

1948   *The Twenty-One Balloons,* William Pene Du Bois
1947   *Miss Hickory,* Carolyn Sherwin Bailey
1946   *Strawberry Girl,* Lois Lenski
1945   *Rabbit Hill,* Robert Lawson
1944   *Johnny Tremain,* Esther Forbes
1943   *Adam of the Road,* Elizabeth Janet Gray
1942   *The Matchlock Gun,* Walter D. Edmonds
1941   *Call It Courage,* Armstrong Sperry
1940   *Daniel Boone,* James Daugherty
1939   *Thimble Summer,* Elizabeth Enright
1938   *The White Stag,* Kate Seredy
1937   *Roller Skates,* Ruth Sawyer
1936   *Caddie Woodlawn,* Carol Ryrie Brink
1935   *Dobry,* Monica Shannon
1934   *Invincible Louisa,* Cornelia Lynde Meigs
1933   *Young Fu of the Upper Yangtze,* Elizabeth Foreman Lewis
1932   *Waterless Mountain,* Laura Adams Armer
1931   *The Cat Who Went to Heaven,* Elizabeth Coatsworth
1930   *Hitty, Her First Hundred Years,* Rachel Field
1929   *The Trumpeter of Krakow,* Eric P. Kelly
1928   *Gay-Neck,* Dhan Gopal Mukerji
1927   *Smoky, the Cowhorse,* Will James
1926   *Shen of the Sea,* Arthur Bowie Chrisman
1925   *Tales from Silver Lands,* Charles Joseph Finger
1924   *The Dark Frigate,* Charles Boardman Hawes
1923   *The Voyages of Dr. Doolittle,* Hugh Lofting
1922   *The Story of Mankind,* Hendrik Willem van Loon

The Nobel Prize for Literature

The most prestigious and lucrative of all literary awards, the Nobel Prize for Literature is given not for a single book, but rather for a complete body of work by a single author. The award is granted to established writers, often at the height of their careers. Funded from money left by Alfred B. Nobel, the Swedish inventor of dynamite, this award is close to $1 million. Administered by the Swedish Academy of Literature, it is an international award given to writers of both prose and poetry.

1994	Kenzaburō Oe (Japan)
1993	Toni Morrison (U.S.)
1992	Derek Walcott (Trinidad)
1991	Nadine Gordimer (South Africa)
1990	Octavio Paz (Mexico)
1989	Camilo José Cela (Spain)
1988	Naguib Mahfouz (Egypt)
1987	Joseph Brodsky (U.S.)
1986	Wole Soyinka (Nigeria)
1985	Claude Simon (France)
1984	Jaroslav Seifert (Czechoslovakia)
1983	William Golding (England)
1982	Gabriel Garcia Marquez (Colombia)
1981	Elias Canetti (Bulgaria)
1980	Czeslaw Milosz (U.S.)
1979	Odysseus Elytis (Greece)
1978	Isaac Bashevis Singer (U.S.)

1977   Vicente Aleixandre (Spain)

1976   Saul Bellow (U.S.)

1975   Eugenio Montale (Italy)

1974   Eyvind Johnson (Sweden)

Harry Edmund Martinson (Sweden)

1973   Patrick White (Australia)

1972   Heinrich Böll (Germany)

1971   Pablo Neruda (Chile)

1970   Aleksandr Solzhenitsyn (U.S.S.R.)

1969   Samuel Beckett (Ireland)

1968   Yasunari Kawabata (Japan)

1967   Miguel Angel Asturias (Guatemala)

1966   Samuel Joseph Agnon (Israel)

Nelly Sachs (Sweden)

1965   Mikhail Sholokhov (U.S.S.R)

1964   Jean-Paul Sartre (France) (declined)

1963   Giorgios Seferis (Seferiades) (Greece)

1962   John Steinbeck (U.S.)

1961   Ivo Andrić (Yugoslavia)

1960   St-John Perse (Alexis St. Léger) (France)

1959   Salvatore Quasimodo (Italy)

1958   Boris Pasternak (U.S.S.R.) (declined)

1957   Albert Camus (France)

1956   Juan Ramón Jiménez (Spain)

1955   Halidór Kiljan Laxness (Iceland)

1954   Ernest Hemingway (U.S.)

1953   Sir Winston Churchill (England)

1952   François Mauriac (France)

1951   Pär Lagerkvist (Sweden)

1950   Bertrand Russell (England)

1949   William Faulkner (U.S.)

1948   T. S. Eliot (England)

1947   André Gide (France)

1946   Hermann Hesse (Switzerland)

1945   Gabriela Mistral (Chile)

1944   Johannes V. Jensen (Denmark)

1943-1940 No award

1939   Frans Eemil Sillanpää (Finland)

1938   Pearl S. Buck (U.S.)

1937   Roger Martin du Gard (France)

1936   Eugene O'Neill (U.S.)

1935   No award

1934   Luigi Pirandello (Italy)

1933   Ivan G. Bunin (Russia)

1932   John Galsworthy (England)

1931   Erik A. Karlfeldt (Sweden)

1930   Sinclair Lewis (U.S.)

1929   Thomas Mann (Germany)

1928   Sigrid Undset (Norway)

1927   Henri Bergson (France)

1926   Grazia Deledda (Italy)

1925   George Bernard Shaw (Ireland)

1924   Wladyslaw Reymount (Poland)

1923   William Butler Yeats (Ireland)

1922   Jacinto Benavente (Spain)

1921   Anatole France (France)

1920	Knut Hamsun (Norway)
1919	Carl F. G. Spitteler (Switzerland)
1918	No award
1917	Karl Gjellerup (Denmark)
	Henrik Pontoppidan (Denmark)
1916	Verner von Heidenstam (Sweden)
1915	Romain Rolland (France)
1914	No award
1913	Rabindranath Tagore (India)
1912	Gerhart Hauptmann (Germany)
1911	Maurice Maeterlinck (Belgium)
1910	Paul J. L. Heyse (Germany)
1909	Selma Lagerlöf (Sweden)
1908	Rudolf Eucken (Germany)
1907	Rudyard Kipling (England)
1906	Giosuè Carducci (Italy)
1905	Henryk Sienkiewicz (Poland)
1904	Frédéric Mistral (France)
	José Echegaray (Spain)
1903	Björnstjerne Björnson (Norway)
1902	Theodor Mommsen (Germany)
1901	René F. A. Sully-Prudhomme (France)

The Pulitzer Prize for Literature

Honoring books that encompass big, often tragic, themes in American life, the Pulitzer Prize has become one of the most popularly recognized book awards. It is named for Joseph Pulitzer, an 1869 immigrant from Hungary, who excelled as a newspaper publisher. When he died in 1911, he left $2 million to Columbia University to administer the prize. Each spring, the winner receives a certificate and $3,000.

1995   *The Stone Diaries,* Carol Shields

1994   *The Shipping News,* E. Annie Proulx

1993   *A Good Scent from a Strange Mountain,* Robert Olen Butler

1992   *A Thousand Acres,* Jane Smiley

1991   *Rabbit at Rest,* John Updike

1990   *The Mambo Kings Play Songs of Love,* Oscar Hijuelos

1989   *Breathing Lessons,* Anne Tyler

1988   *Beloved,* Toni Morrison

1987   *A Summons to Memphis,* Peter Taylor

1986   *Lonesome Dove,* Larry McMurtry

1985   *Foreign Affairs,* Alison Lurie

1984   *Ironweed,* William Kennedy

1983   *The Color Purple,* Alice Walker

1982   *Rabbit Is Rich,* John Updike

1981   *A Confederacy of Dunces,* John Kennedy Toole

1980   *The Executioner's Song,* Norman Mailer

1979   *The Stories of John Cheever,* John Cheever

1978   *Elbow Room,* James Alan McPherson

1977 No award

1976 *Humboldt's Gift*, Saul Bellow

1975 *The Killer Angels*, Michael Shaara

1974 No award

1973 *The Optimist's Daughter*, Eudora Welty

1972 *Angle of Repose*, Wallace Stegner

1971 No award

1970 *Collected Stories*, Jean Stafford

1969 *House Made of Dawn*, N. Scott Momaday

1968 *The Confessions of Nat Turner*, William Styron

1967 *The Fixer*, Bernard Malamud

1966 *The Collected Stories of Katherine Anne Porter*, Katherine Anne Porter

1965 *The Keepers of the House*, Shirley Ann Grau

1964 No award

1963 *The Reivers*, William Faulkner

1962 *The Edge of Sadness*, Edwin O'Connor

1961 *To Kill a Mockingbird*, Harper Lee

1960 *Advise and Consent*, Allen Drury

1959 *The Travels of Jaimie McPheeters*, Robert Lewis Taylor

1958 *A Death in the Family*, James Agee

1957 No award

1956 *Andersonville*, MacKinlay Kantor

1955 *A Fable*, William Faulkner

1954 No award

1953 *The Old Man and the Sea*, Ernest Hemingway

1952 *The Caine Mutiny*, Herman Wouk

1951 *The Town*, Conrad Richter

1950   *The Way West,* A. B. Guthrie, Jr.

1949   *Guard of Honor,* James Gould Cozzens

1948   *Tales of the South Pacific,* James A. Michener

1947   *All the King's Men,* Robert Penn Warren

1946   No award

1945   *A Bell for Adano,* John Hersey

1944   *Journey in the Dark,* Martin Flavin

1943   *Dragon's Teeth,* Upton Sinclair

1942   *In This Our Life,* Ellen Glasgow

1941   No award

1940   *The Grapes of Wrath,* John Steinbeck

1939   *The Yearling,* Marjorie Kinnan Rawlings

1938   *The Late George Apley,* John Phillips Marquand

1937   *Gone With the Wind,* Margaret Mitchell

1936   *Honey in the Horn,* Harold L. Davis

1935   *Now in November,* Josephine Winslow Johnson

1934   *Lamb in His Bosom,* Caroline Miller

1933   *The Store,* T. S. Stribling

1932   *The Good Earth,* Pearl S. Buck

1931   *Years of Grace,* Margaret Ayer Barnes

1930   *Laughing Boy,* Oliver La Farge

1929   *Scarlet Sister Mary,* Julia Peterkin

1928   *The Bridge of San Luis Rey,* Thornton Wilder

1927   *Early Autumn,* Louis Bromfield

1926   *Arrowsmith,* Sinclair Lewis

1925   *So Big,* Edna Ferber

1924   *The Able McLaughlins,* Margaret Wilson

1923   *One of Ours,* Willa Cather

1922   *Alice Adams,* Booth Tarkington

1921   *The Age of Innocence,* Edith Wharton

1920   No award

1919   *The Magnificent Ambersons,* Booth Tarkington

1918   *His Family,* Ernest Poole

The RITA Awards

Romance writing embraces almost half of all mass market fiction sales. This writing is gloried by an award named in honor of the co-founder and first president of Romance Writers of America, Rita Clay Estrada. Although there are many categories, three merit particular mention. In July, winners receive a gold RITA statuette.

Golden Choice Award for Best Romance

1994	*Lord of the Night,* Susan Wiggs
1993	*Come Spring,* Jill Marie Landis
1992	*Outlander,* Diana Gabaldon
1991	*The Prince of Midnight,* Laura Kinsale
1990	*Morning Glory,* LaVyrle Spencer

Single-Title Contemporary Category

1994	*Private Scandals,* Nora Roberts
1993	*This Time Forever,* Kathleen Eagle
1992	*A Man to Die For,* Eileen Dreyer
1991	*Public Secrets,* Nora Roberts
1990	*Private Relations,* Diane Chamberlain
1989	*Leaves of Fortune,* Linda Barlow
1988	*Twilight Whispers,* Barbara Delinksy
1987	*Sunshine and Shadow,* Tom Curtis and Sharon Curtis
1986	*Banish Misfortune,* Anne Stuart
1985	*After All These Years,* Kathleen Gilles Seidel
1984	No award

1983   *Opal Fires,* Lynda Trent

1982   *The Sun Dancers,* Barbara Faith

Single-Title Historical Category

1994   *Untamed,* Elizabeth Lowell (Ann Maxwell)

1993   *Keeper of the Dream,* Penelope Williamson

1992   *Courting Miss Hattie,* Pamela Morsi

1991   *Where Love Dwells,* Elizabeth Stuart (Elizabeth Aubrey Beach)

1990   *The Bride,* Julie Garwood

1989   *Sunflower,* Jill Marie Landis

1988   *The Gamble,* LaVyrle Spencer

1987   *By Right of Arms,* Robyn Carr

1986   *Not So Wild a Dream,* Francine Rivers

1985   *Twice Loved,* LaVyrle Spencer

1984   *Hummingbird,* LaVyrle Spencer

1983   *The Endearment,* LaVyrle Spencer

1982   *Day Beyond Destiny,* Anna James

The Western Heritage Award

To encourage writers to spin tales of the American West, the National Cowboy Hall of Fame and Western Heritage Center created this award. Winners lasso a Wrangler trophy, a bronze sculpture of a cowboy on his horse.

1994   *Pigs in Heaven,* Barbara Kingsolver

1993   *All the Pretty Horses,* Cormac McCarthy

1992   *Set for Life,* Judith Freeman

1991   *Buffalo Girls,* Larry McMurtry

1990   *Broken Eagle,* Chad Oliver

1989   *The Homesman,* Glendon Swarthout

1988   *The Man Who Rode Midnight,* Elmer Kelton

1987   *Heart of the Country,* Greg Matthews

1986   *Playing Catch-Up,* A. B. Guthrie, Jr.

1985   *English Creek,* Ivan Doig

1984   *The Long Riders' Winter,* Frank Calkins

1983   No award

1982   No award

1981   No award

1980   *Hanta Yo,* Ruth Beebe Hill

1979   *Good Old Boys,* Elmer Kelton

1978   *Buffalo Woman,* Dorothy M. Johnson

1977   No award

1976   No award

1975   *Centennial,* James Michener

The Western Heritage Award

1974	*The Time It Never Rained,* Elmer Kelton
1973	*Chiricahua,* Will Henry
1972	*Pike's Peak: A Family Saga,* Frank Waters
1971	*Arfive,* A. B. Guthrie
1970	*The White Man's Road,* Benjamin Capps
1969	*The Buffalo Runners,* Fred Grove
1968	*North to Yesterday,* Robert Flynn
1967	*They Came to a Valley,* Bill Gulick
1966	*Mountain Man,* Vardis Fisher
1965	*Little Big Man,* Thomas Berger
1964	*Honor Thy Father,* Robert A. Roripaugh
1963	*Fire on the Mountain,* Edward Abbey
1962	*The Shadow Catcher,* James D. Horan

The Whitbread Award for Fiction

Unabashed about helping writers increase their book sales, the sponsors of this award include England's Whitbread Plc (the brewer) and the Booksellers Association of Great Britain and Ireland. Winners receive more than $4,000 in November. Whitbread itself foots the bill for a splashy party, press, and public relations for the winning books. The books tend to feature complicated, often surrealistic, and disturbing themes.

1994 *Felicia's Journey*, William Trevor

1993 *Theory of War*, Joan Brady

1992 *Poor Things*, Alasdair Gray

1991 *The Queen of the Tambourine*, Jane Gardam

1990 *Hopeful Monsters*, Nicholas Mosley

1989 *The Chymical Wedding*, Lindsay Clarke

1988 *The Satanic Verses*, Salman Rushdie

1987 *The Child in Time*, Ian McEwan

1986 *An Artist of the Floating World*, Kazuo Ishiguro

1985 *Hawksmoor*, Peter Ackroyd

1984 *Kruger's Alp*, Christopher Hope

1983 *Fools of Fortune*, William Trevor

1982 *Young Shoulders*, John Wain

1981 *Silver's City*, Maurice Leitch

1980 *How Far Can You Go?*, David Lodge

1979 *The Old Jest*, Jennifer Johnston

1978 *Picture Palace*, Paul Theroux

1977 *Injury Time*, Beryl Bainbridge

1976   *The Children of Dynmouth*, William Trevor

1975   *Docherty*, William McIlvanney

1974   *The Sacred and Profane Love Machine*, Iris Murdoch

1973   *The Chip Chip Gatherers*, Shiva Naipaul

1972   *The Bird of Night*, Susan Hill

1971   *The Destiny Waltz*, Gerda Charles

The Whitbread Award for a First Novel

In 1981, Whitbread Plc and the Booksellers Association of Great Britain and Ireland added an award in the category of best first novel. Winners receive a prize of about $4,000 and are further enriched by the help Whitbread renders in promoting their books.

1994   *The Longest Memory*, Fred D'Aguiar

1993   *Saving Agnes*, Rachel Cusk

1992   *Swing Hammer Swing!*, Jeff Torrington

1991   *Alma Cogan*, Gordon Burn

1990   *The Buddha of Suburbia*, Hanif Kureishi

1989   *Gerontius*, James Hamilton Paterson

1988   *The Comforts of Madness*, Paul Sayer

1987   *The Other Garden*, Francis Wyndham

1986   *Continent*, Jim Crace

1985   *Oranges Are Not the Only Fruit*, Jeanette Winterson

1984   *A Parish of Rich Women*, James Buchan

1983   *Flying to Nowhere*, John Fuller

1982   *On the Black Hill*, Bruce Chatwin

1981   *A Good Man in Africa*, William Boyd

Above the Rest

Special recognition is given here to books that have outperformed the rest by receiving more than one honor.

Four Awards
Billy Bathgate, E. L. Doctorow

Three Awards
All the Pretty Horses, Cormac McCarthy
The Counterlife, Philip Roth
Love Medicine, Louise Erdrich
Rabbit Is Rich, John Updike
The Stone Diaries, Carol Shields

Two Awards
An Artist of the Floating World, Kazuo Ishiguro
Beloved, Toni Morrison
Bootlegger's Daughter, Margaret Maron
Breathing Lessons, Anne Tyler
The Collected Stories of Katherine Anne Porter, Katherine Anne Porter
The Color Purple, Alice Walker
The Confessions of Nat Turner, William Styron
Crossing the River, Caryl Phillips
A Disaffection, James Kelman
The Dispossessed, Ursula K. Le Guin
Doomsday Book, Connie Willis
Dreamsnake, Vonda McIntyre
Dune, Frank Herbert
Empire of the Sun, J. G. Ballard
Ender's Game, Orson Scott Card

A Fable, William Faulkner
The Fixer, Bernard Malamud
The Folding Star, Alan Hollinghurst
Foreign Affairs, Alison Lurie
The Forever War, Joe Haldeman
The Fountains of Paradise, Arthur C. Clarke
G, John Berger
Gateway, Frederik Pohl
The Gods Themselves, Isaac Asimov
The Good Earth, Pearl S. Buck
Goodbye, Columbus, Philip Roth
Gravity's Rainbow, Thomas Pynchon
The Handmaid's Tale, Margaret Atwood
Ironweed, William Kennedy
The Left Hand of Darkness, Ursula K. Le Guin
Lost in the City, Edward P. Jones
The Mambo Kings Play Songs of Love, Oscar Hijuelos
Midnight's Children, Salman Rushdie
Neuromancer, William Gibson
On the Black Hill, Bruce Chatwin
Pigs in Heaven, Barbara Kingsolver
Rabbit at Rest, John Updike
Remembering Babylon, David Malouf
Rendezvous with Rama, Arthur C. Clarke
Ringworld, Larry Niven
The Satanic Verses, Salman Rushdie
The Shipping News, E. Annie Proulx
Speaker for the Dead, Orson Scott Card
Startide Rising, David Brin
The Stories of John Cheever, John Cheever
A Summons to Memphis, Peter Taylor
A Thousand Acres, Jane Smiley
Wartime Lies, Louis Begley
World's End, T. Coraghessan Boyle

Calendar of Awards

February

The Caldecott Medal

The Newbery Medal

March

The Ernest Hemingway
Foundation Award

The National Book Critics Circle
Award

The Western Heritage Award

April

The Edgar Allan Poe Award

The PEN/Faulkner Award

The Nebula Award

The Pulitzer Prize for Literature

May

The Howells Medal (presented
every five years)

The Sue Kaufman Prize for First
Fiction

The Agatha Award

June

The ABBY Awards

July

The RITA Awards

September

The Hugo Award

October

The James Tait Black Memorial
Prize

The Booker Prize

The Nobel for Literature

November

The *Los Angeles Times* Book
Prize

The National Book Award

The National Jewish Book Award

The Whitbread Award for Fiction

The Whitbread Award for a First
Novel

Author Index

Note: Page numbers are followed by the year the award was granted in parentheses.

Author Index

Author Index

Field, Rachel, 14 ('45), 37 ('30)
Finger, Charles Joseph, 37 ('25)
Fischer, Tibor, 9 ('93)
Fish, Helen Dean, 14 ('38)
Fisher, Vardis, 49 ('66)
Fitzgerald, Penelope, 7 ('79), 10 ('88, '90)
Flanagan, Thomas, 30 ('79)
Flavin, Martin, 44 ('44)
Fleischman, Paul, 35 ('89)
Fleischman, Sid, 35 ('87)
Flynn, Robert, 49 ('68)
Follett, Ken, 15 ('79)
Forbes, Esther, 37 ('44)
Forester, C. S., 5 ('38)
Forster, E. M., 6 ('24)
Forsyth, Frederick, 16 ('72)
Fox, Paula, 36 ('74)
France, Anatole, 40 ('21)
Francis, Dick, 15 ('81), 16 ('70)
Friedman, Russell, 35 ('88)
Freeling, Nicolas, 16 ('67)
Freeman, Judith, 48 ('92)
Freeman, Mary E. Wilkins, 20 ('25)
Fremlin, Celia, 16 ('60)
Fuchs, Daniel, 31 ('80)
Fuller, John, 52 ('83)

Gabaldon, Diana, 46 ('92)
Gaddis, William, 25 ('76, '94)
Gaines, Ernest J., 30 ('93)
Galsworthy, John, 40 ('32)
Gammell, Stephen, 12 ('89)
Garcia, Cristina, 28 ('92)
Gardam, Jane, 50 ('91)
Gardner, John, 30 ('76)
Garfield, Brian, 16 ('76)
Garnett, David, 6 ('22)
Garwood, Julie, 47 ('90)
Gee, Maurice, 4 ('78)
George, Jean Craighead, 36 ('73)
Gibbons, Kaye, 23 ('88)
Gibson, William, 21 ('85), 33 ('85)
Gide, André, 40 ('47)
Gilb, Dagoberto, 18 ('94)
Gilchrist, Ellen, 25 ('84)
Gjellerup, Karl, 41 ('17)
Glasgow, Ellen, 20 ('40), 44 ('42)
Goble, Paul, 13 ('79)
Golding, William, 4 ('79), 7 ('80), 38 ('83)
Goldman, Francisco, 23 ('93)
Goldreich, Gloria, 31 ('79)
Gordimer, Nadine, 4 ('71), 8 ('74), 38 ('91)
Grade, Chaim, 31 ('78), 32 ('67)
Grau, Shirley Ann, 43 ('65)
Graves, Robert, 5 ('34)
Gray, Alasdair, 50 ('92)
Gray, Elizabeth Janet, 37 ('43)

Greenberg, Joanne, 32 ('64)
Greene, Graham, 5 ('48)
Greenfield, Robert, 31 ('83)
Grove, Fred, 49 ('69)
Gulick, Bill, 49 ('67)
Gunesekera, Romesh, 9 ('94)
Gunn, Neil M., 5 ('37)
Gurganus, Allan, 23 ('90), 24 ('91)
Gurnah, Abdulrazak, 9 ('94)
Guterson, David, 17 ('95)
Guthrie, Jr., A. B., 44 ('50), 48 ('86), 49 ('71)

Hader, Berta, 14 ('49)
Hader, Elmer, 14 ('49)
Hagedorn, Jessica, 28 ('90)
Haien, Jeannette, 23 ('87)
Haldeman, Joe, 22 ('76), 33 ('76)
Haley, Gail E., 13 ('71)
Hall, Adam, 16 ('66)
Hall, Donald, 12 ('80)
Hall, Radclyffe, 5 ('26)
Hallahan, William, 15 ('78)
Hamilton, Jane, 18 ('89)
Hamilton, Virginia, 36 ('75)
Hamsun, Knut, 41 ('20)
Handforth, Thomas, 14 ('39)
Hansen, Mark Victor, 1 ('95)
Hardy, Ronald, 4 ('62)
Hartley, L. P., 5 ('47)
Hart, Carolyn, 2 ('88, '93)
Hauptmann, Gerhart, 41 ('12)
Hawes, Charles Boardman, 38 ('24)
Hazzard, Shirley, 30 ('80)
Heinemann, Larry, 25 ('87)
Heinlein, Robert A., 22 ('56, '62, '67)
Helprin, Mark, 31 ('81)
Hemingway, Ernest, 39 ('54), 43 ('53)
Henriquez, Robert, 5 ('50)
Henry, Marguerite, 36 ('49)
Henry, Will, 49 ('73)
Herbert, Frank, 22 ('66), 34 ('66)
Hersey, John, 32 ('50), 44 ('45)
Hesse, Hermann, 40 ('46)
Hewat, Alan V., 18 ('86)
Heyse, Paul J. L., 41 ('10)
Higgins, Aidan, 4 ('66)
Hijuelos, Oscar, 29 ('89), 42 ('90)
Hill, Ruth Beebe, 48 ('80)
Hill, Susan, 51, ('72)
Hillerman, Tony, 16 ('74)
Hodges, Margaret, 12 ('85)
Hogrogian, Nonny, 13 ('66, '72)
Hollinghurst, Alan, 3 ('94), 9 ('94)
Holtby, Winifred, 5 ('36)
Hope, Christopher, 9 ('92), 50 ('84)
Horan, James D., 49 ('62)
Hudson, Jeffery, 16 ('69)

Author Index

Author Index

Title Index

Note: Page numbers are followed by the year the award was granted in parentheses.

Title Index

Title Index

Title Index

Lies of Silence, 10 ('90)
Life & Times of Michael K, 7 ('83)
The Light of Day, 16 ('64)
Like Water for Chocolate, 1 ('94)
Little Big Man, 49 ('65)
The Little House, 14 ('43)
The Little Island, 14 ('47)
Lincoln: A Photobiography, 35 ('88)
The Lingala Code, 16 ('73)
Lon Po Po: A Red-Riding Hood Story from
    China, 12 ('90)
Lonesome Dove, 42 ('86)
The Long Goodbye, 16 ('55)
The Long Night of White Chickens, 23 ('93)
The Long Riders' Winter, 48 ('84)
The Longest Memory, 52 ('94)
Lord of Light, 22 ('68)
Lord of the Night, 46 ('94)
The Lost Father, 10 ('88)
The Lost Girl, 6 ('20)
Lost in the City, 18 ('93), 28 ('92)
Love in the Time of Cholera, 24 ('88)
Love Medicine, 23 ('85), 24 ('85), 30 ('84)

Madeline's Rescue, 14 ('54)
The Macguffin, 28 ('91)
Make Way for Ducklings, 14 ('42)
The Magic Barrel, 26 ('59)
The Magic of Blood, 18 ('94)
The Magnificent Ambersons, 45 ('19)
The Mambo Kings Play Songs of Love,
    29 ('89), 42 ('90)
The Man in the High Castle, 22 ('63)
Man Plus, 33 ('77)
A Man to Die For, 46 ('92)
The Man Who Rode Midnight, 48 ('88)
The Man with the Golden Arm, 27 ('50)
The Mandelbaum Gate, 4 ('65)
Maniac McGee, 35 ('91)
Many Moons, 14 ('44)
Mao II, 17 ('92)
Maps to Anywhere, 18 ('91)
The Masters, 4 ('54)
The Matchlock Gun, 37 ('42)
Mating, 25 ('91)
Maus II, A Survivor's Tale: And Here My
    Troubles Began, 24 ('92)
May I Bring a Friend, 13 ('65)
M.C. Higgins the Great, 36 ('75)
Mei Li, 14 ('39)
Memoirs of a Fox-Hunting Man, 5 ('28)
Memoirs of a Midget, 6 ('21)
Memory of Autumn, 32 ('69)

Men at Arms, 5 ('52)
The Middle Age of Mrs. Eliot, 4 ('58)
Middle Passage, 25 ('90)
The Middleman and Other Stories, 30 ('88)
Midnight's Children, 3 ('81), 7 ('81)
Miracles on Maple Hill, 36 ('57)
Mirette on the High Wire, 12 ('93)
Miss Hickory, 37 ('47)
Miss Mole, 5 ('30)
Missing May, 35 ('93)
Mr. Mani, 31 ('93)
Mr. Sammler's Planet, 26 ('71)
Mrs. Frisby and the Rats of NIMH, 36 ('72)
Mom Kills Kids and Self, 18 ('80)
Monkey, 5 ('42)
Monsieur, or The Prince of Darkness, 4 ('74)
The Moon Is a Harsh Mistress, 22 ('67)
Moon Tiger, 7 ('87)
Morning Glory, 46 ('90)
Morte D'Urban, 26 ('63)
Moses Supposes, 28 ('94)
The Mosquito Coast, 3 ('81)
Mother and Son, 4 ('55)
Mountain Man, 49 ('66)
The Moviegoer, 26 ('62)
My Glorious Brothers, 32 ('49)
My Old Sweetheart, 23 ('83)

Naked Once More, 2 ('89)
Neuromancer, 21 ('85), 33 ('85)
The New Man, 4 ('54)
New Orleans Mourning, 15 ('91)
Nice Work, 10 ('88)
Nights at the Circus, 3 ('84)
Nine Days to Christmas, 13 ('60)
No Enemy but Time, 33 ('83)
Noah's Ark, 13 ('78)
North to Yesterday, 49 ('68)
The Northern Light, 29 ('87)
Not So Wild a Dream, 47 ('86)
Now in November, 44 ('35)
Number the Stars, 35 ('90)

O, My America!, 31 ('81)
October Light, 30 ('76)
Offshore, 7 ('79)
Old Bones, 15 ('88)
The Old Devils, 7 ('86)
The Old Forest..., 17 ('86)
The Old Jest, 50 ('79)

Title Index

Title Index

Title Index